THE MONUMENTAL MYSTERY ON THE National Mall

First Edition ©2018 Carole Marsh/Gallopade International/Peachtree City, GA
Current Edition ©February 2019
Ebook edition ©2018
All rights reserved.
Manufactured in Peachtree City, GA

Carole Marsh Mysteries™ and its skull colophon are the property of Carole Marsh and Gallopade
International.

Published by Gallopade International/Carole Marsh Books. Printed in the United States of America.

Managing Editor: Janice Baker
Assistant Editor: Beverly Melasi-Haag
Cover Design: Randolyn Friedlander
Content Design: John Hanson

Gallopade International is introducing SAT words that kids need to know in each new book
that we publish. The SAT words are bold in the story. Look for this special logo beside each
word in the glossary. Happy Learning!

*Gallopade is proud to be a member and supporter of these educational organizations and
associations:*

American Booksellers Association
American Library Association
International Reading Association
National Association for Gifted Children
The National School Supply and Equipment Association
The National Council for the Social Studies
Museum Store Association
Public Lands Alliance
Association of Booksellers for Children
Association for the Study of African American Life and History
National Alliance of Black School Educators

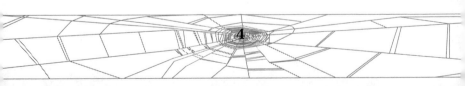

Once upon a time ...

Hmm, kids keep asking me to write a mystery book. What shall I do?

Mimi

Papa said ...

Why don't you set the stories in real locations?

That's a great idea! And if I do that, I might as well choose real kids as characters in the stories! But which kids would I pick?

MiMi, PiCK ME, PiCK ME!

Avery

PAPA, TELL MiMi TO PiCK ME!

Sadie

MiMi, ME TOO!

Ella

MiMi, DON'T FORGET ME!

Evan

Pick me!

We can go on the *Mystery Girl* airplane ...

I CAN FLY US ANYWHERE!

Or aboard the *Mimi*!

Take me to the Forbidden City!

Or by surfboard, rickshaw, motorbike, camel ...!

I can put a lot of **history, MYSTERY, SCIENCE,** legend, lore, and **laughs** in the books! It will be educational and fun!

Good stuff!

9

Can I apply?

And so, join Mimi, Papa, Avery, Ella, Evan, and Sadie aboard the *Mystery Girl*—where the adventure is real and so are the characters!

START YOUR ADVENTURE TODAY!
www.carolemarshmysteries.com

1

A CAPITAL IDEA

"I smell bacon!" Ella sat up in bed and rubbed her still-sleepy eyes. "And is that maple syrup, too?" She hopped out of bed and hurried downstairs toward the tantalizing aromas coming from the kitchen.

The now-familiar breakfast scene made her smile. Ella and her sisters, Avery and Sadie, plus her brother, Evan, had been staying with their grandparents for a week of their summer vacation.

Mimi and Papa stood at the stove. Mimi, clad in her bright red jogging outfit, busily flipped her special animal-shaped pancakes. Papa wore his chef's hat and a white apron over his lucky blue shirt and crisp jeans.

Ella started to say "Good morning," but stopped short when Avery and Evan stormed into the kitchen like twin tornadoes circling each other.

"Give me that camera right now!" Avery shouted. Her blue eyes blazed with anger.

"Aww, come on. I just got it for my birthday," Evan replied, his blue eyes twinkling mischievously as he dodged her outstretched hands.

Papa turned from the stove and stepped between them. "Whoa there, little pardners. It's a mite too early in the morning to be makin' such a big ruckus."

"He started it!" Avery wailed. "He took a picture of me with his digital camera when my mouth was full of toothpaste!"

Papa sat down at the table, and held his arms out to Sadie, his youngest granddaughter. She scrambled into his lap and buried her head against his shoulder. "You two have just about scared the daylights out of your little sister. Now settle down and eat some breakfast." He fixed a stern gaze on Evan. "And you, young man, will not use your camera to aggravate your sister again. We must always respect one another's privacy."

Mimi gave Evan "the look." No one could deliver "the look" better than Mimi. Evan knew it was time to apologize. "You're right, Papa," Evan said, glancing sideways at Avery. "I'm sorry," he said. Avery squinted at her brother and murmured, "Just don't do it again, little bro."

The sound from the television in the family room flowed into the kitchen. The news anchors chatted about the upcoming Fourth of July celebration on the National Mall in Washington, D.C. The programming switched to a live broadcast from the nation's capital. Mimi looked up as Ella walked by on her way to the table.

"Turn that up, dear," Mimi said. She wiped her hands on a towel and drew closer to the television. The face of a woman with short dark hair and vivid blue eyes filled the screen. She smiled broadly as she answered questions about the celebration.

"Well, look at that!" Mimi exclaimed. "That's Olivia Carson! I haven't seen her in years! Shush! Let's hear what she's up to."

"I am very honored to be this year's Celebration Ambassador," Olivia remarked. "We've had a remarkable find this year. A very rare painting was discovered in the Lockkeeper's House during its recent move. The Lockkeeper's House is the oldest building on the National Mall. It's really a shame it's no longer open to the public."

A faded painting of three men silhouetted alongside Independence Hall in Philadelphia appeared on the TV screen. The words "We the People" were emblazed across the top of the painting, with the Declaration of Independence in the background.

The camera then focused on Olivia discussing the painting. "Historians believe," she explained, "that it was painted around the time the Declaration of Independence was signed."

Evan jumped in front of the television screen and snapped a quick picture of the painting.

"Hey! Get out of the way!" everyone shouted at once.

Olivia's interview continued. "Look," she said, "even the clock on Independence Hall is still visible." She pointed to the clock and laid a hand over her heart. "It's a miracle," she remarked, "that this painting survived without the proper preservation. It positively gives me goosebumps to think about it! But soon it will be safely tucked away in its rightful home—the Smithsonian Castle on the National Mall."

In another part of town, someone else was getting goosebumps just thinking about the plans they had for that painting. And phase one of those plans was already underway!

2

IT'S ALL ON THE MALL

Mimi turned to the family, her eyes wide with excitement. "Papa, get my purse. We're going to Washington, D.C.! I'm calling my friend Olivia right now to make all the arrangements."

Mimi grabbed her cell phone and started tapping numbers. "I needed to gather research for my latest mystery book set in Washington, D.C., so this is perfect timing." She fanned herself with her credit card. "I can't wait to show you kids the sights on the National Mall!"

SMACK! Avery and Ella raised their right hands in a high-five. "Love those mystery-writing trips!" Avery exclaimed. Mimi, a famous children's mystery book author, often brought her grandchildren along on her journeys to research books. Over the years, the kids had learned to share their grandmother's love of history.

Evan rose abruptly from his seat. He stacked his plate noisily in the dishwasher and semi-slammed its door. "Ohhhh man, does that mean I have to go shopping all day in some mall with the girls?" he whined.

"No, Evan," Mimi reassured him. "It's not that kind of mall. The National Mall is actually a state park."

"Here, Mimi," Avery suggested, handing her phone to her grandmother. "Use my locator app to show us."

The app opened, and Mimi traced a tree-lined area with her finger. "The National Mall takes up two miles of the downtown area. It is often called our nation's 'front lawn.' It extends from the U.S. Capitol to the Lincoln Memorial."

Mimi rotated the phone to make a wider screen. "See? Our nation's most well-known monuments and museums are all in one place."

DING! They were interrupted by an email arriving on Mimi's phone. She returned Avery's phone and picked up her own. "Well, I wonder what this could be?" she asked with a sheepish grin. She opened the email and showed everyone a confirmation for airline tickets to Washington, D.C.

"We're going tomorrow?" Ella asked. When Mimi nodded, the kids high-fived each other once again.

"This is awesome," Avery said. Then she suddenly looked serious. "What am I going to wear?"

"One of your million outfits," Ella replied, rolling her eyes.

"I just love flying on planes," Evan remarked, "especially if they have TV screens for all the seats."

Sadie was still sitting on Papa's lap. "Am I going too?" she asked, not really knowing what the excitement was all about.

Papa lowered her to the floor. "You betcha, little filly."

Throughout the flight, the kids peppered Mimi with questions about the National Mall. Soon, Ella created a game to see who could think up the hardest question to ask her.

"Here's one for you, Mimi," Ella said. "How old is the National Mall? "

Mimi thought for a minute. "Hmmm...," she murmured. "I think the National Mall could actually be considered a work in progress because the building process has continued over two hundred years." She tapped her chin with her finger. "I know it started with the White House in 1800. And before you ask, no, I didn't know that because I was there when the White House was built!" She peeked over her red sparkly glasses at Evan, who giggled at her comment.

Mimi pulled a pamphlet out of her purse that showed a timeline of when the structures along the National Mall were built. "See?" she asked. "The Capitol was built in 1829 and it goes on and on." She slid her finger along the timeline until she reached the end. "The newest building was built in 2016. It's the National Museum of African American History and Culture."

"Here's a question," Avery said. "How did the National Mall get its name?"

Mimi threw up her hands. "OK, you got me. And now I must resort to my trusty tablet." Mimi swiftly researched her answer. "It is believed," she explained, "that the National Mall was named after the playing field used in a popular British game during the late 1700s. The field was called 'pall mall.' The playing field was rectangular and called a 'mall.' The parcel of land designated for the park was similar in shape so was later dubbed the National Mall."

"What is the most interesting fact you know about the National Mall?" Evan asked.

Mimi's eyes twinkled. "What I find most interesting," she replied, "is that the National Mall connects—as well as separates—the Capitol from the White House. She wiggled her eyebrows at the kids.

As the plane made its descent, they got their first glimpse of the magical Washington,

D.C., skyline beneath them. The majestic buildings gleamed bright white against the darkening sky. "Oh my gosh, there's the White House!" Avery shouted. "It's so beautiful. And now I can see the Lincoln Memorial too!"

"Look, there's the Capitol Building," Ella exclaimed, pointing out the window. "I had no idea it was so big!" As the last shimmering rays of the sun fell over the horizon, turning day into night, Ella saw the Washington Monument's colossal tower looming in the distance. "This is going to be a great trip," she said softly to herself. "So much history; so much to do!"

3

SECRET SYMBOL

"I'm so happy to see you again!" With a shriek of laughter, Olivia pulled Mimi into a big bear hug. "We're going to have so much fun, and look who I brought with me." Olivia held her hand out to a young girl about Ella's age. Her wavy dark hair was pulled back into a ponytail. "This is my daughter, Jilly."

Jilly wore jeans and a bright red-and-white-striped shirt. She stepped forward shyly and waved at the kids. She turned to Mimi with clasped hands. "I've read all your books, Mrs. Marsh."

"Why thank you, Jilly," Mimi said. "I always love meeting a fan." She introduced Avery, Ella, Evan, and Sadie to Jilly and then found a few empty tables nearby. "Let's all sit for a minute while Papa finds the shuttle to our hotel."

Jilly sat down at one of the tables and the kids quickly joined her. Almost immediately, Evan's stomach started growling. He fidgeted in his chair, embarrassed because he thought Jilly had probably heard the grumbling. "I'm hungry," he announced.

Ella rolled her eyes. "So what else is new?" she said.

Evan ignored his sister. "Mimi, can I go get a snack?" he pleaded.

Mimi pushed her carry-on bag under the table to give them more room. "Yes, but don't be gone long, and stay within sight of our table. This airport is big, and I don't want to go looking for you. Take Ella with you, dear."

Ella swung around in her chair so fast that her long brown hair wrapped around her neck. "Wait...what?? What did I do?!"

Ella grumbled, but took Evan by the hand. The two wandered to a snack bar offering fresh fruit and cookies.

"Oh, yeah. That's what I want!" Evan said.

"It all looks delicious," Ella observed. "I'll get enough for all of us." While she paid for the food, Evan watched all the people bustling around the airport.

Suddenly, Evan had the strangest feeling he was being watched. He quickly scanned the area. He thought he saw someone peep around a column across the room, then dart behind it again. It looked like a young woman. He waited to see if she would poke out her head once again.

Oh, there, she did it again, Evan thought. And this time, their eyes met. He was close enough to see that she had short red hair and wore red-rimmed glasses. The look on her face proved that she was up to something. But what? Evan took a step forward.

The woman turned and briskly walked away. Evan tried to snap a picture of her, but it came out blurry.

"Hey, wait!" Evan called, but the young woman kept on walking. As she moved between tables, the ID badge clipped to her belt caught on a chair. The elastic band holding the badge stretched as far as it could. SNAP! The ID badge tumbled to the floor, but the young woman kept going.

After waiting a few minutes for the woman to come back and retrieve her badge, Evan took matters into his own hands. He scooped up her ID badge from the floor. It contained no name, only a five-digit number in the upper right corner and an unusual gold symbol in the center. It was useless to try to find the young woman now, so he slipped the ID badge into his backpack just before Ella reached him.

"Evan!" Ella ran up to him. "What are you doing?"

But Evan's thoughts were elsewhere. *Who is that young woman, and why is she spying on me?*

Ella came to stand in front of him. "Didn't you hear me call you?" she asked her brother.

"No; sorry, Ella," he said, but his mind was racing. *We just got here, and I think we might be onto a new mystery,* he thought.

The family headed outside to find the airport shuttle to their hotel. But inside the airport, the young woman with the red-rimmed glasses crawled under tables frantically searching for her ID badge.

4

SECRET STUFF

"Rise and shine, kiddos!" Papa shouted through the door to the kids' hotel room. Despite the moans and groans coming from inside the room, the kids got ready for breakfast in less than an hour.

As the family walked to the elevator, Evan asked, "Can we go swimming in the hotel pool after breakfast, Mimi? I hear they have the coolest indoor pool and waterslide anywhere!" He wore a green t-shirt, a pair of jeans and flip flops. His new camera hung precariously around his neck.

Ella waited hopefully for Mimi's answer. She looked like a ray of sunshine in her yellow tank top, yellow shorts, and yellow sandals.

"Oh, I think that can be arranged," Mimi said with a smile.

"YESSSS!" Ella and Evan shouted. Evan pulled his elbow down sharply in a fist pump.

Avery trailed the group, busily scrolling her thumb along the surface of her cell phone. She was dressed in a red-and-white, polka-dotted shirt, blue jean cutoffs, and white sunglasses. Her long blonde hair was pulled into a ponytail. "What's everyone so happy about this morning?" she asked as she caught up to her siblings.

"Mimi's letting us go to the hotel pool after breakfast," Evan told her. "It has a HUMONGOUS waterslide!"

Avery wasted no time researching the hotel pool on her phone. When she saw the size of the slide, she stopped in her tracks and gasped. "Are you two kidding me?" she exclaimed, shoving the phone under Evan's nose to show him.

"What?" Evan said. "Are you chicken?"

Avery lowered her sunglasses and peered at her brother with piercing blue eyes. "No, I'm not chicken, Evan." She walked by and ruffled his blonde hair. "Just smart."

DING! The elevator arrived, and as the family was getting in, Evan spied a small piece of bright yellow paper behind a potted plant. He grabbed the paper and stuffed it into a pouch on the side of his backpack. The door to the elevator closed, and they all went down to breakfast.

Mimi, Papa, and the kids entered the hotel dining room the same time as Olivia and Jilly did. The tables were dressed with snow-white tablecloths topped with fresh flowers.

As they sat down to eat, a man entered the dining room. He wore a pink jacket over a dark purple shirt. His brown snakeskin shoes creaked when he walked. With his dark hair formed into an edgy pompadour, he was striking and odd all at the same time. Everyone wondered who he was.

To everyone's surprise, the man stopped at their table. Evan bent sideways in his seat and snapped a picture of the man's shoes.

"Hello, Ms. Carson," he said in a deep, melodious voice. "I am Alfred Tablebottom."

"Why, Mr. Tablebottom, it is so nice to meet you in person," Olivia remarked. "I would like to introduce you to my dear friends and their three grandchildren." She laid her hand gently on her daughter's shoulder. "And this is my daughter, Jilly."

Alfred Tablebottom shook Mimi's and Papa's hand. "It is a pleasure to meet all of you." He motioned with his hand, and a young woman came to his side. "I would like to introduce you to my assistant, Tara."

Evan rubbed his eyes in disbelief. Tara was the young woman he had seen in the airport! He started to open his backpack to return her ID badge, but the look in her eyes begged for his silence.

"So nice to meet you, Tara," Olivia said. She turned to Mimi and Papa. "Mr. Tablebottom has been commissioned by the Smithsonian

Castle on the National Mall. He's going to make a few minor repairs to the historic painting before its unveiling."

"Exactly," Mr. Tablebottom said. "Ms. Carson, if you have a few minutes after breakfast, I'd like to go over some details about the painting and the celebration." He checked his watch. Let's say about eleven o'clock?"

"That will be fine," Olivia replied. "Will Tara be joining us?"

"Well I..." Tara started to say, nervously.

"I see no need for Tara to join us at this time," Mr. Tablebottom said. "Do you, Tara?" he asked with a smile that didn't quite match his cold blue eyes. She had been assigned to him by the Smithsonian while he repaired the historic painting. He was annoyed by the way she seemed to watch his every move.

"No, not at all," Tara agreed. Thoughts raced through her mind as she stared at Evan. *How could I have let this happen? I had a secret, and now this boy holds the key.*

As Tara and Mr. Tablebottom started to leave, she narrowed her eyes at Evan. The look she gave him chilled him to the bone. *Why did she look at me like that?* he thought.

Ella glanced at Evan just as Tara looked his way. Ella gasped when she saw the menacing look on Tara's face. *What was that all about?* she thought. *I need to ask Evan about that as soon as we're alone!*

5

A MONUMENTAL MYSTERY

As they entered the atrium of the hotel's indoor pool and waterslide area, Evan could not contain his excitement. "This is the best hotel ever!" he shouted. "Look at the size of that slide!" All eyes were glued to the towering, super-loop slide that ended in a deep, crystal-clear pool.

The girls were **aghast** at the sheer size of it. Avery whispered to Ella, "I think that monster slide may have teeth."

"I think you may be right," Ella whispered back.

Evan waved his hands up and down. "Oh yeah, I am so going on that!" he exclaimed.

"Count me out," Avery announced. "I don't need that kind of excitement, thank you very much." She tossed her towel on a deck chair and wandered over to the hot tub shaped like a giant shell. "But I'll be right here to watch over you two." She twisted her hair atop her head and secured it with a clip.

Now that they were alone for a moment, Ella saw her chance to speak with Evan. "Hey," she whispered, "Evan, I need to ask you something."

"Later," Evan said. He scurried to the pool, intending to do a cannon ball into the water near Avery. But he slipped on the deck instead. His planned cry of "Whooo Hooo!" turned into "Whooooooah!" as he tumbled into the water.

Hearing Evan's cry, Avery jumped out of the hot tub in an instant. But Ella made it to the side of the pool first to check on their brother. She stuck out her hand to help pull him out. "Are you OK?" she asked. At his nod, she added, "You are very lucky, little brother, that you didn't bust that thick skull of yours."

Avery was relieved to see that Evan wasn't hurt. "Did you not notice the sign that says, "NO RUNNING!?" she asked.

"Yeah, I get it. And I'm sorry," Evan replied. He raked his fingers through his wet blonde hair and started to walk away.

Avery stared after him and put her hands on her hips. "Hey, Evan," she called, "you're heading in the wrong direction if you're still going on that monster waterslide." She motioned behind her.

"I've decided to go on it later," Evan said sheepishly. "Listen, there's something I want to show you two." He walked over to the umbrella table and reached for his backpack on the deck chair.

Ella watched her brother. She was convinced that something odd was going on with him. When she and Avery joined Evan, she looked deep into her brother's eyes. "So little brother, spill it," she ordered.

Evan looked both ways, and when he huddled in, they did too. "It all starts with this lady in the airport with red-rimmed glasses," he began. When Evan finished his story, he told the girls about the ID badge. "First, she's running away from me like I'm a spider," he described. "Then, at the hotel with Mr. Tablebottom, she acted all shy and everything."

"Yes," Ella said. "She seemed very shy right up until they were leaving." She looked at her brother. "I saw the look she gave you, Evan. It was creepy! That's why I wanted to talk to you. There's a mystery going on here, and I'm going to find out what it is."

DING! Avery received a text on her phone, so she moved away to let Ella and Evan talk in peace and quiet.

Evan turned to pull Tara's ID badge out of his backpack to show his sisters when Ella said, "What's that sticking out of your backpack?"

"What? Where?" Evan reached for his backpack.

"Here," Ella said, as she tapped the bottom of a half-zipped pouch. A yellow piece of paper popped out and landed on the table.

"Oh, that," Evan said. "I found it on the floor by the elevator.

Ella unfolded the paper and read, "3014 and 3016."

Avery walked back to the table and snatched the paper from Ella's hand. "What's this?" she asked. "Oh, you wrote down our room numbers so you wouldn't forget them? How cute is that?!" She ruffled his hair, and walked away to answer another text.

Ella stared at Evan. "Why would someone want our room numbers?" she asked. "This is really strange. Let's keep our eyes and ears open," she suggested, and stuffed the paper back in the pouch.

Suddenly, Papa's booming voice filled the pool area. "Hey, kids, it's time for your afternoon vittles!" He tipped his Stetson back off his forehead. "I hear this here hotel is cooking up a mess of barbecued steaks, hamburgers, and fries. Who's up for that?"

"Yes, it's time to eat," Mimi announced as she entered the atrium with Sadie. "But Papa and I will be enjoying the chicken salad, won't we, dear?" she said, patting his hand.

"I suppose," Papa mumbled with a grimace.

"Will Jilly and her mom be there, too?" Ella asked.

"Yes," Mimi said. "I'm so happy you kids made her feel welcome. She is very shy and doesn't have any sisters or brothers."

"Hmmm, fancy that," Avery said, shooting a glance at Evan. "I bet she doesn't have to worry about anyone taking her picture when she's brushing her teeth!"

6

THE POOL IS COOL

"Look at all the food!" Evan said, as the family entered the picnic area set up for the hotel barbecue. Everything else was forgotten when he spied the buffet table loaded with platters and bowls.

Mimi and Papa helped carry plates overflowing with delicious salads, hamburgers, steaks, vegetable kebobs, and seafood. "Here Evan, try a hush puppy," Mimi said, placing a small, round, deep-fried morsel on his plate.

"Hush puppy?!" He looked at Mimi suspiciously. "What is that?"

"Oh, Evan, you are too much!" Mimi said with a laugh. "Hush puppies are made from cornmeal and then deep fried. We eat them all the time in the South." She popped one in her mouth. "Folklore says that a fisherman's hungry dogs wouldn't stop yapping for his catch, so he threw them cornmeal battered fritters to 'hush the puppies.' "

"Ok, I'll eat one," Evan said, "but I better not bark like a dog later."

"Woof!" said Ella.

Olivia rushed up to the table. Her cheeks were flushed pink. "I'm so sorry I'm late. Mr. Tablebottom and I spent quite a busy morning together." She sat down next to Mimi. "I didn't know there was so much to do to get a painting moved to the Smithsonian. And now I'll be tied up this afternoon as well." She patted Mimi's arm. "I'm sorry; really I am."

"Oh pish-posh," Mimi said with a flick of her wrist. "Don't worry about me. We're planning to tour the National Mall this afternoon, anyway. But I have an idea. Would you mind if Jilly hangs out with us?"

Olivia glanced at her daughter sitting with the kids. "Oh, could she? That would be wonderful," she said with a smile. "How about it, Jilly? Would you like to spend the day with the kids?"

"Yes, ma'am!" Jilly answered quickly. Evan celebrated with another enthusiastic fist pump.

Jilly turned to Ella. "When Mother said you were going on a tour of the National Mall, I really wanted to go, too," she confessed. "Even though I grew up around here, it's always fun to share the experience with others. Plus, I know a lot about all the monuments and memorials and museums, so I can answer lots of questions!"

"That would be great!" Ella said. "So how does it work? Do you pick a tour of the monuments you want to see?"

"The National Mall is a very big area," Jilly explained. "It does help to know what you want to see," she said. "Oh, and you'll want to have your cameras out every minute."

"I can do that!" Evan said, patting his beloved camera.

Ella snapped her fingers. "I know," she suggested. "Let's put our heads together and decide what places we most want to visit. Then, we can ask Mimi if we can plan our tour around those choices."

"OK," Avery said, as she scrolled up and down on her phone. "I want to see the Lincoln Memorial."

Wiping a bit of mustard from her chin, Ella said, "I want to see the Capitol."

"The Air and Space Museum is my favorite," Jilly added.

"That leaves you, Evan," Ella said. "What do you want to see?"

Evan paused for a minute. "I'd like to see the Lincoln Memorial Reflecting Pool," he blurted out. "I heard it's really cool!"

Jilly thought a second, then frowned. She looked up the reflecting pool on her phone. "Ah, Evan, I have sad news for you. The pool was recently drained to kill parasites that were harming the ducks swimming in it."

"Really? Yuck!" Evan said. He frowned and crossed his arms over his chest. "But I still want to see it."

When she saw the look on Evan's face, she tried to cheer him up. "Don't worry though; it says here that once the pond is squeaky clean again, they'll refill it with water."

"When's that going to be?" Evan asked, exasperated. He had come all this way to see the reflecting pool, and it didn't even have any water in it!

Jilly continued to scroll down the web page. "Check this out," she announced. "It says here that the cleaning will be completed before the July Fourth Celebration."

"That's great!" Ella said. She was glad her brother would get to see the reflecting pool with water in it. As the family headed to the hotel shuttle for their afternoon at the National Mall, no one saw Tara dart into a nearby elevator. She was still trying to find her missing ID badge.

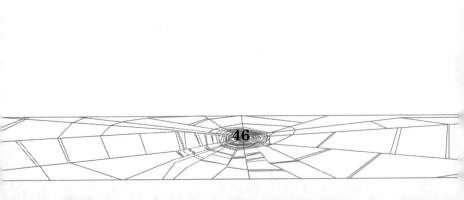

7

MEETING GEORGE

The minute the hotel shuttle arrived at the National Mall's zero milestone, the kids jumped out of their seats, ready to pounce. Papa quickly stood up, towering above the children in his black cowboy boots and Stetson hat. "Hold it right there, partners," he warned.

Mimi moved in front of the kids to talk to them. "We are going to get on the National Mall tour bus in a minute, but have you all decided what you'd like to see?"

"We have!" Ella said. She rattled off the places the kids had discussed at lunch. "Can we go to those places, Mimi?"

"But of course," Mimi said. "Papa and I discussed visiting the very memorials you wanted to see. So, we have reserved the perfect two-day tour for us." She gestured to a shiny red bus waiting by the curb.

When the kids crossed the street to get the bus, they were surprised to see a man dressed like George Washington standing beside it. He wore a white wig, dark blue coat, tan waistcoat, and white knee britches tucked into knee-high, black leather riding boots.

"Oh, how fun!" Ella laughed. "Mimi, you are too much!"

"No way!" Evan exclaimed as he started snapping pictures. "My friends are never going to believe this!" He ran up and took several selfies with George Washington.

Mimi smiled. "President Washington and I met on my last trip to Washington D.C.," she said.

The general gave a quick tug on the lapels of his uniform. "Aye, I remember it well, Madam," he said, bowing low before her.

"All aboard!" the driver of the tour bus shouted.

"Madam?" President Washington took Mimi's arm and guided her up the steps of the bus. Papa carried Sadie behind them. Avery, Ella, Evan, and Jilly followed and quickly found seats. The rest of the passengers boarded the bus, and the tour got underway.

"Good afternoon, everyone," the driver announced. "My name is Bill, and I'd like to welcome you to our tour of the National Mall." As Bill pulled out into traffic, he described the places they'd visit. The kids followed along in the pamphlet the tour company had provided.

"Many historians say there is no person in American history who had a greater impact on America than George Washington," Bill remarked. "We are honored that he could join us on our tour today to talk about the National Mall." He handed his microphone to the man in the George Washington costume. "They're all yours, President Washington."

"Good afternoon, my fellow patriots," the speech began.

As George Washington began his speech, Avery leaned forward in her seat and stole a sideways glance at Ella. "I know he isn't really George Washington," she whispered, "but he could be his twin." She held up her phone to show Ella a portrait of America's first president. "Here, look."

Ella peered at the portrait. Sure enough, the two men looked amazingly alike. "Wow! How is that even possible?" she whispered back.

"The National Mall," George Washington said, as he gestured to the area around him, "is a national park of memorials and monuments to celebrate the key chapters in American history. It contains several of the Smithsonian museums, as well as art galleries, cultural institutions, memorials, sculptures, and statues."

He paused, as if remembering something from the past. "But it wasn't always so," he remarked. "This area started out as lowlands along the Potomac River that were prone to flooding."

Avery and Ella looked at each other in surprise. "It's so hard to imagine what this place looked like before all the beautiful monuments were built," Ella whispered. Avery nodded in agreement.

Bill's voice boomed over the loudspeaker. "Now, we invite you to watch a short video." A colorful map filled the television screens while George Washington began his narration. "The National Mall is a national park that covers more than one thousand acres. It stretches from the Lincoln Memorial on the west to the U.S. Capitol Building on the east.

"In 1790," he continued, tugging on his lapels, "I chose this land as the site for our new nation's capital. I commissioned a French engineer named Pierre L'Enfant to plan the city of Washington, D.C., including the National Mall. The whole task was quite an amazing undertaking!"

George Washington sighed heavily. "But the War of 1812 made life in Washington most unpleasant for a time. British forces stormed the city in 1814, burning the partially completed U.S. Capitol and other buildings. They even set fire to President Madison's house!" He shook his head and cleared his throat. "So sorry, but that always gets to me. However, the president's house was rebuilt, painted white, and was known forever after as the White House!"

The bus halted at the curb, and Bill took over the tour. "Thank you, President Washington, for your interesting facts." As George Washington took a bow, the tourists began to applaud and cheer. Evan stood up in his seat, put two fingers in his mouth, and whistled loudly. "You tell 'em, Evan!" Ella exclaimed with a giggle.

"Well, folks," Bill continued, "this is our first stop, the United States Capitol. It was designed by an architect named William Thornton after he won the competition to design the Capitol. It stands 288 feet high, with the Statue of Freedom crowning its top. And..." he paused, "the Capitol is where history is made every day." He pushed a lever, and the doors opened. "Have fun, and we'll see you back here at three o'clock sharp!"

As everyone filed off the bus, Avery lingered for a minute to text one of her friends back home. As she moved up the aisle to the exit, she noticed a red piece of paper folded in half sticking out from under a seat. She picked it up, unfolded the handwritten note and read:

KIDS IDENTIFIED.
WILL KEEP THEM IN SIGHT.

Avery gasped. *Is that note about us? And who wrote it?* Her mind began to race. *I need to show this to the others!* She stuffed the note into the pocket of her shorts and ran to catch up with her family.

8

THE HOUSE ON CAPITOL HILL

As they stood on the bottom of the steps leading up to the Capitol building, Mimi clapped her hands together in delight. "So, are you all ready to walk into a living monument, where the U.S. Congress and Senate meet?"

"YESSSS!" the kids shouted.

Ella stared up at the Capitol. *It is sooooo huge*, she thought. *It's where big political decisions are made every day. I'm so small in comparison. And yet, because I am an American, someone small like me can still step up and be heard!*

The kids climbed the steps to the Capitol. Mimi, Papa, and Sadie took the elevator.

Excited for her new friends, Jilly said, "Wait until you see the inside. It's huge, and there's so much to see and do!" They joined Mimi and Papa near the Welcome Center and moved into Emancipation Hall. Mimi and Papa stopped to ask a guide some questions. The kids wandered around nearby.

Ella couldn't believe her eyes. "This place is so beautiful and so big!" She looked around, wide-eyed. "There must be thousands of people in here!"

"It seems like it, doesn't it?" Jilly remarked. "On average, the Capitol sees from three to five million visitors each year from all over the world."

"Whoa!" Avery said and then stopped in her tracks. Without another word, she lowered her sunglasses to look at the giant white statue in front of them. "Who's that lady?"

Jilly stood next to the huge sculpture. "This," she motioned with her hand, "is the Statue of Freedom. She was the original plaster mold for the bronze statue that has stood on top of the Capitol since 1863. She is almost 20 feet tall."

Avery couldn't take her eyes off the Statue of Freedom. She wore a military helmet encircled with stars, and her curly hair flowed down her back. The helmet was topped with an eagle's head and feathers. Talons hung down either side of her face like earrings. Her flowing gown was gathered at the chest by a brooch with the letters "US" engraved on it. She was draped in a fur-trimmed robe.

"That is the most interesting statue I have ever seen," Avery exclaimed.

"Look at this!" Evan pointed at Freedom's right hand. It lay on the hilt of a sheathed sword. "Is that wayyyy cool or what?"

"Oh my gosh, look at this," Ella added. She stared at Freedom's left hand, which held a wreath and a striped shield. "Avery, can I borrow your phone for a minute?"

Avery punched in her password and handed it to her sister. "Thank you," Ella said. She looked up the wreath and the shield. "Oh, it says here," she explained, "that the wreath is called a 'laurel wreath of victory,' and this shield is the shield of the United States. It has 13 stripes to represent the original 13 colonies."

Ella handed Avery her phone. "I really like all the symbology," Ella remarked. *It is so like America, with beauty and strength together.*

As the family got on the escalator heading up to the Crypt, no one saw Tara storm through the front doors of the Capitol, not far behind them.

9

COLONIAL CRYPT

With so much to explore and so little time left, the kids hurried to enter the room called the Crypt. Mimi and Papa strolled along with Sadie, reading about the 13 statues representing the original 13 colonies.

"Aw, man," Evan complained. "I was hoping for gloomy tunnels and scary mummies and stuff in here." But the Crypt was quite the opposite. To their surprise, it was a brightly lit space full of statues and documents in glass cases. The room itself was round, with rows of columns supporting the floor above it.

Avery decided to do some research on her phone. "It says there are forty of these columns in this room bracing the Rotunda upstairs," she said.

"Oh look," Ella called as she ran to the center of the room. "There's a big starburst on the floor," she said. "Why is it here?"

"That's an easy one," Jilly said. "It represents the center of the Capitol, and the center of Washington, D.C."

"So why the creepy name for this room?" Avery asked, looking around. Nothing looked scary to her.

"Well," Jilly said sheepishly. "There's a room below this starburst that was intended to be the crypt where George Washington was buried. It was designed so tourists could look through the hole in the floor here to see his coffin below."

"EEEWWWW!!!" Ella cried, jumping off the star. She grabbed her **abdomen**. "I think I'm going to be sick. I was actually standing over George Washington's grave."

"But there's no body," Jilly reminded her.

"So," Avery said, "if he's not here, then where is he?"

"George Washington wanted to be buried at Mount Vernon," Jilly explained. "So, this area in the floor was sealed up. But the empty crypt is still down below us."

Papa's voice echoed through the columns. "OK, pardners," he said, "time to head upstairs to the Rotunda!"

When the family got off the elevator, Ella spotted a blue, folded piece of paper lying in the corner. She snatched it up quickly and read the note:

OBJECT NOT FOUND!

"Hmmm," she said. "Don't know what that's about." She stuck the note in the pocket of her shorts and ran to catch up with the others.

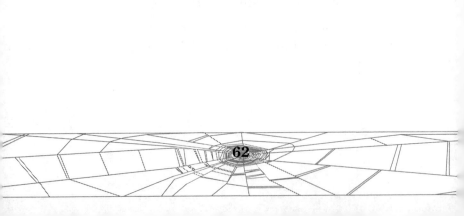

62

10

STAR-SPANGLED SPIES

As they entered the Rotunda, the kids were amazed by the HUGE dome above them. "Hey, want to know something cool?" Jilly asked. The kids all nodded. She pointed up to the dome. "This Rotunda is totally made of cast iron and weighs nine million pounds. And," she said, "if you took the Statue of Liberty off her pedestal, she would fit into this room."

Evan twirled in a circle while he looked up, up, and up, until he had to crane his neck to see so high. "What's up there?" he asked, pointing up. "I can't make out what it is."

Jilly looked up too. "It's hard to see, but that's a painting of George Washington ascending into heaven. And sitting in the circle with him are the 13 colonies," she said, pointing to the very top of the dome. "It's actually called the Apotheosis of Washington."

Avery typed "Apotheosis of Washington" into her phone. She found a picture and showed it to Evan. "See?" Avery asked. "It was painted in 1865. Washington is flanked by Liberty and Victory, and those are Greek and Roman gods on the outer circle."

Evan was still craning his neck and spinning to see it all. Suddenly, he felt dizzy, and the room started to whirl. He tripped over his feet and tumbled backward into a sculpture of three people in a gathering. "Oops!" he said as he landed in the lap of one of the statues.

Ella, Avery, and Jilly rushed over to help him. "Are you OK?" Ella asked.

"I think so," Evan said. He was deeply embarrassed, and his cheeks were bright red.

Ella gave him a high-five. It wasn't fair to bait her brother when he was down. *Well, maybe a little*, she thought. "Leave it to you to be today's entertainment," she said with a smile. Come on. Let's catch up with the others."

When they approached, Mimi and Papa were listening to a tour guide explain a painting of George Washington laying the cornerstone of the U.S. Capitol in 1793. Avery and Jilly had moved along to view another painting. Evan tugged on Papa's hand. "Psst, I gotta go to the bathroom," he whispered.

Papa motioned with his head. "Go ahead and go." He turned back to the painting, then around again. "On second thought," he added, "Ella, please go with Evan. I don't want him wandering too far."

Evan and Ella looked around the area but didn't see any restroom signs. They found a door marked "Employees Only" where they thought they might find someone who knew where to find a bathroom. They quickly slipped through the door, finding themselves in a dimly lit, narrow hallway between two buildings.

It was chilly, and Ella shivered. She could hear the steady drip, drip, drip of water from somewhere deep within. She rubbed her arms, partly from the creeps, and partly from the cool of the cement walls all around them. "Ah, Evan," she remarked, "I don't think this is the way to the restroom."

But Evan's attention was captured by something else. "Wow!" he said, staring at the stairs before them. As his gaze followed them upward, the steps seemed to zig-zag into infinity. Evan pulled a mini flashlight out of his backpack and started up the stairs. He stopped on a landing.

"Hey, Ella, this must be some sort of secret stairway!" Evan shouted. As he moved away from the landing, the light from his flashlight grew dimmer and dimmer. He headed up another set of stairs and stopped on another landing. "Come on, Ella, it's really cool!" He went up several more steps and flashed the light down over the rail at her. He was already about twenty feet higher than his sister.

Ella stood in the same spot with the beam of light shining directly in her eyes. She folded her arms across her chest. "Evan!"

she shouted in frustration, her voice vibrating through the stairwell. "I'm sure those stairs go really high, but I personally don't care to find out how high. Its creepy in here!" She shuddered at the thought of being left alone at the bottom any longer.

Evan glanced out a small window that overlooked the Rotunda below. "Hey, there's Avery and Jilly!" He watched as his sister stopped with Jilly to look at a painting. Suddenly, he caught some movement out of the corner of his eye. He spied a tall, broad-shouldered man with black hair moving toward his sister. The man wore a dark suit and sunglasses.

"What is going on?" Evan whispered. Now, the man was standing within a few feet of Avery! He turned aside, and spoke into his watch. Evan scanned the crowd and saw a blonde man wearing similar sunglasses and a dark suit standing near the exit door. He was talking into his watch too.

"OK, Ella, I'll be right down," Evan said quickly. He didn't want to frighten Ella by telling her someone was spying on their sister, but they had to hurry.

"What?" Ella put her hands on her hips. "Just like that?" She narrowed her eyes at him. "All right, what's going on? Since when do you give in so easily?"

Evan didn't answer her. He wanted to warn Avery. Turning, he leaped back down the stairs. *What if I can't get to Avery in time?* he thought. Without a word, he grabbed Ella by the hand and ran until they were standing once again in the dimly lit hallway. Evan dropped his flashlight as he hurried to get away.

When the children came storming through the door, Mimi exclaimed, "There you are! Where on earth have you two been?"

Evan shuffled his feet. "Ah, well, we just made a wrong turn on the way to the bathroom, went up and down some stairs, and turned down a hall that led back here."

Mimi ruffled his hair. "Well, we're all together again. That's what matters."

When Mimi and Papa went to look at another exhibit, Avery laid her hand on Ella's shoulder. "Is that really what happened?" she whispered. "You both look flushed."

Ella wasn't exactly sure what had happened either. "More or less," she said with a shrug.

"Uh-huh." Avery raised her eyebrows. She turned and spotted Evan drinking out of a water fountain. She decided to try her luck with him instead. "OK, little brother, what just happened that has you looking like you want to jump out of your skin?" She folded her arms across her chest and planted her feet to show Evan that she'd stand there until he answered.

Evan swiped the back of his hand over his lips to wipe away drops of water. He looked left and right. "Well, there were these two men," Evan blurted out. "I think they're spying on us. Well, they were spying on you and Jilly a little while ago, but I think maybe they're really watching all of us."

Avery quickly spun around and scanned the crowd for anyone suspicious. She stomped her foot in frustration. *I knew I should have told the others about that clue I found on the bus, but I just haven't had the time.*

Evan's face suddenly went pale. "What is it?" Avery asked. "You look like you've just seen a ghost."

Evan glanced toward the escalator. "Look, at the top of the escalator. It's those two guys who were spying on you and Jilly!"

"Hey, kid, wait!" The blond man shouted when he saw Evan.

Avery grabbed Jilly by the hand while Ella grabbed Evan's arm. As they hurried along, Avery barked orders at them. "Here's the deal," she said. "Two men are following us for some reason," she told the group. "Let's split up. Don't run, but walk quickly, and everyone double-back to Mimi and Papa. Got it?"

"Yes!" they all agreed.

"Let's go!" Avery yelled.

The kids took off in four different directions. The two men looked confused as to which way to go first. They finally set their sights on Evan but retreated when they heard Mimi call, "Yoo-hoo, kids! Are you ready to head back to the bus?"

The four kids practically ran her down as they skidded to a stop next to her and Papa. He was carrying Sadie, who had decided to take a nap instead of look at statues.

In a hallway, the two men threw up their hands in defeat and started talking into their watches.

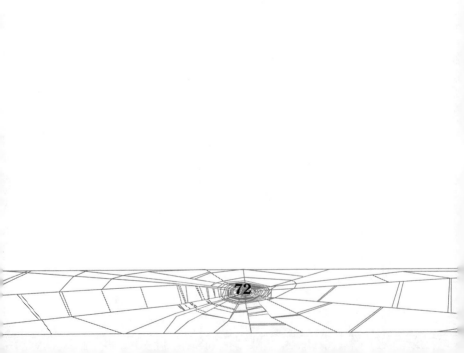

11

BAFFLED ON THE BUS

Before the men could pursue them again, the kids headed quickly to the exit. They raced down the steps of the Capitol to the tour bus, way ahead of Mimi, Papa, and Sadie. They showed their passes and boarded the bus, hurrying down the aisle to the back. Ella practically pushed Avery into a seat, then sat next to her. The kids all slumped down in their seats just below eye level of the window in case the men were looking for them.

"What just happened back there in the Capitol?" Ella whispered breathlessly.

"I'm not sure," Avery panted. "But I'm starting to wonder if it has something to with that ID badge Evan has." Before they could discuss anything further, Mimi, Papa, and Sadie boarded the bus.

Mimi plopped down in her seat across the aisle from them and started fanning herself with a Capitol tourist brochure. "Whew, it's so hot outside!" she said. She looked across the aisle at Ella and Avery. "Why did you kids run out of the Capitol like that?" She leaned forward a little and turned her head slightly to see all four kids. "And why are you all slumped down in your seats like that?"

Avery and Ella immediately pushed themselves upright. "Oh, we're just a little tired from running," Ella said. "We were racing to see who could run down the Capitol steps the fastest. You know, to get exercise."

"Uh-huh." Mimi eyed her granddaughters over the rim of her sunglasses, but she let it go at that...for now. Instead she sat back to relax, enjoy the tour, and let the air conditioner blow cool air on her face.

Avery leaned in and whispered to Ella, "Mimi didn't believe a word of that story, you know."

As they sat waiting to leave, the blond-haired man boarded the bus. He stood silently, scanning the seated passengers as if looking for someone.

Ella was talking to Avery but fell silent as she saw him. She gripped her armrest tightly and hunkered down in her seat. Fearful, she elbowed Avery's arm. "Avery!" she hissed.

Avery was texting one of her friends. She shoved Ella's arm away. "Quit it, Ella." When Ella elbowed her again, Avery said, "Gosh, what is it?"

Ella's voice quivered. "One of the men who was spying on us in the Capitol just got on the bus," she whispered. "It's Mr. Blondie. I think he's looking for us!"

They heard Evan gasp from the seat behind them. He saw the man too. In a squeaky voice, Evan whispered, "He's gonna see me and come get me!"

Avery could hear fear in his voice. "No, he's not, Evan. Now listen to me, both of you," Avery said quietly. "Stay calm and stay low. Mimi and Papa are right across the aisle.

They would never let anyone get past them to get us." She shook her sister's arm. "Ella, focus, and take a quick peek into the aisle, and see what he's doing now."

Ella slid her head slightly sideways to see around the seat in front of her. Mr. Blondie spoke quietly to the driver as he handed him something. Then he exited the bus. Ella let out the breath she'd been holding. "The coast is clear. He got off the bus," she announced.

"Are you sure?" Evan asked. His voice sounded muffled as the top of his blond head popped up slightly between the seats.

"Yes, I'm sure," Ella said.

Shortly after, Bill the driver spoke over the loudspeaker. "Hello, folks. I hope you all enjoyed your time at the Capitol. We'll be underway in a few minutes. In the meantime, is there someone by the name of Evan on the bus? If so, please come forward and claim your flashlight. A gentleman said you dropped it, and he wanted to return it to you."

Evan knew his trembling legs wouldn't carry him long enough to walk up the aisle and claim his flashlight. He was still too scared. His fingers crept slowly around Ella's seat and tapped her on the shoulder, startling her. "What!...Who?" She turned around and saw Evan's big blue eyes staring back her.

"Will you get my flashlight for me?" he asked.

"OK, but next time, just ask, instead of scaring me to death," Ella replied. When she reached the driver, she held out her hand to receive the flashlight.

"Are you Evan?" Bill asked.

"No," Ella replied. She couldn't help but giggle. "I'm his sister."

"Well, I guess it's OK to give his flashlight to you." He smiled, handing it to her.

"Yes, thank you, sir," she said, turning to return to her seat.

"Oh, wait," Bill said, taking a small, folded piece of bright green paper out of his top pocket. "The gentleman also left this for Evan." He held it out to her in the palm of his hand.

"Thanks," Ella said. Her fingers seemed to **oscillate** before plucking the note from his hand. She slipped it into her pocket to show Evan later. She didn't think he could take seeing a note from a spy right now.

Once Ella was seated, Bill announced, "Our next stop on the National Mall is the Air and Space Museum." Everyone on the bus cheered and clapped. Bill closed the doors, tooted the horn, and they were underway.

Ella sat back and looked out the window at the tree-lined street. After the stress of seeing Mr. Blondie enter the bus with Evan's flashlight, spending time at the Air and Space Museum was going to be a calm end to a wild afternoon. Or so she thought.

12

A WORLD OF AIR AND SPACE

As the bus made its way to the National Air and Space Museum, the overhead monitors played a video. Bill's voice came over the speakers. "The National Air and Space Museum was opened on the National Mall in 1976," he explained. "And by 2016, it was named one of the most visited museums in the world!"

The video featured a stunning aerial view of the museum. "This outstanding museum is filled with historic artifacts, airplanes, rockets, and spacecraft that showcase America's history of aviation and space flight."

"Space flight, that's for me!" Evan exclaimed. He had recovered from his earlier scare and was ready for the excitement of visiting the National Air and Space Museum.

When the video ended, Bill pulled the bus over to the curb and opened the door. "Don't forget, folks," he said. "The bus will be here to pick you up this evening at six o'clock sharp. Enjoy the National Air and Space Museum."

A tall tower with sparkling starbursts near the top stood near the entrance. Evan stepped off the bus and stood in front of it. He looked up, shading his eyes to block the blinding sun reflecting off it. His blue eyes grew wide in amazement. His gaze traveled so high he was almost bent over backwards trying to follow the lines to the top. He stepped back slightly and bumped into a short metal post near the curb. "NOoooooo!" he cried.

Avery had just stepped off the bus when she heard Evan cry out. She saw him fall with a thud and land on his behind. She hopped down, grabbed her brother's arm, and tugged him to his feet. "Are you OK?"

Evan brushed some tiny bits of gravel from the back of his shorts. "I'm OK. I just wanted to see to the top. Look how high it is!"

Papa brushed some dust from the back of Evan's shirt. "Hey little pardner, do you think you can maybe refrain from any more stunts for a while? We're not even inside yet!"

Once inside, Evan's eyes gazed upward again. They had entered the Milestones of Flight Hall where historic aircraft hung from the soaring ceiling. "WOW!!!" Evan's voice echoed around the gallery lined with massive windows from floor to ceiling. "Look at the size of this place!" The girls were awestruck by the enormity of the gallery and the history laid out before their eyes.

Papa pointed out the bright orange Bell X-1, his favorite aircraft in the gallery. "One of my heroes named Chuck Yeager broke the sound barrier in that airplane," Papa said. "That was quite a day in history!"

An elderly man wearing a Yankee Air Force hat stood quietly nearby. He looked at

Evan and motioned at an airplane with *Spirit of St. Louis* written on it. "Young man, that aircraft is my favorite," he remarked. "A great man named Charles Lindbergh flew that plane across the Atlantic Ocean in 1927. It was the first solo flight across that big ocean, and quite an **intrepid** feat in those days. He changed the world for all of us pilots who came after him."

Papa nodded and shook the man's hand. "You are absolutely right, sir. And thank you for your service, Joe." The man tipped his hat in response.

As the elderly man walked away, Evan said, "How did you know his name, Papa?"

"It was engraved on his belt buckle," Papa said with a chuckle. "That is a wise old gentleman, yesiree."

The kids continued to walk through the myriad of hallways, rooms, and galleries in the museum. A shiny spacecraft caught Avery's eye. She pointed to the craft as she read the sign. "This one is the Mercury *Friendship 7*. It says that on February 20, 1962, astronaut

John Glenn was the first American to orbit the Earth three times in this capsule. The flight lasted just under five hours."

"I am so glad you noticed that spacecraft," Mimi said. "The space program was very new back in 1962. So, the older spacecraft did not land at the Kennedy Space Center in Florida like you may have seen the space shuttle do. The space capsule was attached to the tip of a giant rocket ship, and launched into outer space," she explained. "When it came back to Earth, the capsule reentered the atmosphere hooked to a parachute, and plunged in the ocean. Then a U.S. Navy ship recovered the capsule and the astronauts."

Mimi turned to the kids. "I'm glad these space capsules are here. We should never forget our pioneer astronauts. They were incredibly brave to do things that had never been done before." She clasped her hands together. "Oh, I must have a picture of all of you with the Mercury capsule." The group huddled together, and since Papa had the longest arm, he took the selfie. "One, two, three...selfie!"

Mimi wanted to stop at the souvenir shop to look for a space capsule key chain. "Can we walk around a little bit more?" Avery asked.

"Of course," Papa said, taking Sadie's hand. "There's not much time before the bus leaves, so meet us back here."

The kids continued to be fascinated by each display they saw. When they came to the display from the first moon landing on July 20, 1969, Evan was awestruck. He shouted, "Ella, get a picture of me touching this moon rock!"

At the next display, he stopped to take a picture of a space toilet, and a shadow fell over him. He aimed his camera in the direction of the shadow. He thought it was one of his sisters creeping up behind him. But when he started clicking, he saw Mr. Blondie! Just then, a rush of people came off the elevator, and Evan disappeared into the crowd.

Evan quickly found the girls, and together they hurried to find Mimi and Papa.

"Outsmarted by a kid!" Mr. Blondie growled. He spoke gruffly into his watch. "Come on, let's get back to the office."

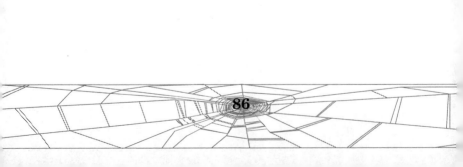

13

CREEPY CLUES

Back at the hotel, the kids were exhausted from their day at the Capitol and National Air and Space Museum. Mimi and Papa had taken Sadie to get pizza. Avery, Ella, Evan, and Jilly searched the kitchen for snacks and drinks. Avery put some cookies on a tray and carried it to the table. Ella and Jilly followed with tall glasses of lemonade.

"I'm glad your mom called Mimi and said you can stay with us overnight," Ella told Jilly.

"Me too!" Jilly said.

The group sat at the table, each wrapped up in their own activities. Avery texted on her phone. Jilly read a book on her tablet. Evan looked at the brochure he had picked up in the musuem. Ella sat quietly in her chair, pensively crunching chocolate chip cookies.

Everything was jumbled in Ella's head. She was sure there was a mystery here, but the pieces were just not adding up. Maybe what they needed to do was start back at the beginning.

"I have an idea," Ella suggested. "While Mimi and Papa are gone, let's talk about what went on yesterday and today, and think things through."

Avery, Jilly, and Evan stopped what they were doing and looked at Ella. She took a sip of her lemonade. "Let's start with yesterday," she started. "Evan saw a woman spying on him at the airport. When she discovered that he saw her, she quickly walked away. She was wearing an ID badge that snapped off her belt when it snagged on a chair. Evan picked it up and put it in his backpack. This morning, Evan found a note with our room numbers on it."

"Here," Evan said as he handed her the bright yellow sticky note with room numbers on it. Ella placed it in the center of the table. They huddled in and looked at it like they expected it to leap out at them. No one seemed willing to break the silence.

"Well..." Avery said loudly. All the kids jumped in their seats. "What?" she asked, as the kids looked at her wild-eyed.

"Not funny," Ella said, brushing cookie crumbs off her chin. "You startled me so bad I nearly bit off my tongue taking a bite of my cookie."

"I am sorry," Avery said, "but Evan's note just reminded me that I also found a note."

"What? Where?" Ella asked.

"When we were getting off the sightseeing bus," Avery replied. She stood and stuck her hand in the pocket of her jean shorts. She pulled out a crumpled red sticky note and read it:

KIDS IDENTIFIED.
WILL KEEP THEM IN SIGHT.

She tossed it onto the table with the yellow note.

"You've had a clue all this time and you didn't say anything?" Ella cried. "Of all the—" she started to say, but stopped in mid-sentence. She reached into the pocket of her shorts and pulled out a piece of blue paper. "Oops," she said and opened it.

OBJECT NOT FOUND!

"And wait," she said as she pulled the green note out of her other pocket. "I'm sorry! That bus driver named Bill handed me this note when he gave me Evan's flashlight. I didn't want to upset Evan anymore, so I put it in my pocket and forgot about it."

Ella unfolded the note and read it:

I'LL SEE YOU AT THE LINCOLN MEMORIAL!

Ella looked at the other kids. "What does that even mean?" No one knew. The clues all lay in disarray on the table. "Hmmm... Ella said. "They're a pretty rainbow of colors, wouldn't you say?" She looked up at the others. "I wonder if it's relevant."

"Don't overthink things, Ella," Avery said, taking a bite of a cookie. "It'll just make your head hurt." Ella glared at her sister.

Jilly stacked the notes in order on the table. She looked at Evan. "Do they always talk to each other that way?" she asked.

"Sometimes, I guess," he answered. "But most of the time, they're getting after me about something," he added with a smile.

Avery began to pace. "I think it's weird that they seem to know where we are—anywhere we are," she said. "Wait! Maybe that ID badge has some sort of tracking device on it! Let me see it, Evan."

"OK, sure." Evan began to root around inside his backpack for the ID badge. But just as he put his hand on it, the door opened. In came Mimi and Papa with a stack of warm pizzas. Sadie proudly carried a bag of delicious-smelling breadsticks. Quickly, Evan forgot everything he was doing, and the ID badge remained buried at the bottom of his backpack.

14

MEMORIAL MAYHEM

"How are my little pardners this morning?" Papa's booming voice echoed through the hotel suite as he entered the kitchen.

"Fine," Evan mumbled through a mouthful of cereal.

Papa looked around. "Where are the girls?"

Evan held his spoon near his mouth. "Doing girlie things in their room," he said, then shoveled in another mouthful of cereal.

Papa looked at his watch. "Well they best hurry up. We need to catch the shuttle to the sightseeing bus."

"Here we are, Papa!" Avery, Ella, and Jilly breezed into the kitchen, talking and laughing.

As Avery reached for a cereal box, she asked, "So where are we going today, Papa?"

"We are going to the Lincoln Memorial," he replied.

Avery suddenly dropped the cereal box, spilling its contents onto the floor. Evan spewed the cereal he had in his mouth across the table. Ella sprang to her feet, tipping her glass of water over into a plate of toast and onto the floor. Jilly tossed a nearby towel to Papa to help clean up the mess.

"Thank you, Jilly," Papa said, quickly mopping up the table. He stared at the kids. "What in tarnation is wrong with all of you this morning? You're all acting like someone's yappin' at your heels."

"Good morning to youuuu!" Mimi strolled into the kitchen holding Sadie's hand. Sadie was dressed in a pretty red, white, and blue sundress. Mimi wore her red shorts and a white top that said "I Love Washington, D.C." in rhinestones. She stared at the disaster dripping from the table to the floor and at all of them cleaning it up. "Oh my, what happened here?"

"Nothing," the kids and Papa all said in unison.

"All righty then," she said cheerfully. "Is everyone ready to go?"

The kids hurried to the sightseeing bus ahead of Mimi and Papa. They were anxious to sit together to talk about the mystery clues. Evan rounded the front of the bus to the driver's side and came to a screeching halt. Standing beside the door was a very tall man with a beard, wearing a very tall hat. Evan had to crook his neck way back just to see him. "Hi, where's George Washington?" Evan wanted to know.

"Oh, he's been gone for many years now," the man replied. "Perhaps I can be of assistance. My name is Abraham Lincoln."

When everyone was seated on the bus, Bill announced, "Next stop is the west end of the National Mall—and the Lincoln Memorial!

And who better to fill you in on the details of that incredible historic monument than Abraham Lincoln himself. He served as the sixteenth President of the United States until his assassination in 1865. He wrote the Gettysburg Address and helped pass the 13th Amendment to abolish slavery. President Lincoln, the floor is all yours."

Mr. Lincoln stood at the front of the bus and took a bow. "Good morning, ladies and gentlemen," he began. "The Lincoln Memorial is a very special place to me. I am very honored that the government created a memorial to remember my time as your president.

"You see," he continued. "I started out my life on a small farm in Kentucky. Back then, we didn't have much formal education. All that I learned, I taught myself by reading books. I mastered the Bible, Shakespeare, and English and American history. Later, I became a lawyer by teaching myself once again. I got into politics, and in 1860, I was elected President of the United States."

Avery took out her cell phone and looked up images of Abraham Lincoln. "Wow! See, Ella? He looks just like the real Abraham Lincoln. Where do they get these guys?"

But Ella was distracted and stayed silent. *How did Mr. Blondie know where they'd be today? What do he and his partner want?* Then she paused to ponder some wisdom she had learned from her mystery-writing grandmother. *What does Mimi always say about solving a mystery? "Look past the red herrings and focus."*

The bus hit a bump and Abraham Lincoln had to fight to keep his hat on. Avery and Jilly giggled. President Lincoln righted his hat. "Ahem," he said. "Where was I? Oh, yes. The design of the Lincoln Memorial was inspired by the Greek Temple of Zeus. It opened in 1922 and has often been the site of civil rights speeches and protests. And in 1963," he added, "Dr. Martin Luther King Jr. made his famous 'I Have a Dream' speech on the Memorial steps."

"Thank you, President Lincoln," Bill said. Everyone applauded and cheered. Bill pulled into the bus area of the Lincoln Memorial and opened the door. "Have a wonderful time!"

15

SUPERB STATUE

Avery's phone dinged. She read the message and looked up from her phone. "Uh-oh, little brother. I just received a newsfeed about the Lincoln Memorial Reflecting Pool." She pulled up a search engine and quickly found a live broadcast about the breaking news.

"Lemme see," Evan said, reaching for Avery's phone.

"As you know," the news reporter explained, "the Lincoln Memorial Reflecting Pool was recently drained for cleaning. A drone flying overhead to film the event captured a mysterious symbol on the bottom of the pool." The camera panned over the massive reflecting pool to show a large disk in the center. The middle of the disk showed a fountain bubbling over, feeding into three separate branches forming a dotted pinwheel.

Evan handed the phone back to Avery. The news reporter began to speak again, but Evan didn't hear him. His ears were buzzing. *I know I've seen that symbol before. But where?*

"Earth to Evan," Ella said, waving her hand in front of his face.

"Yeah, what's up?" Evan asked, as if in a daze.

Ella lowered her head until her eyes were within inches of his face. "You are getting off the bus and going on this tour with us, right?"

"Oh, yeah, sure." Grant shook his head to clear it. He'd think about the mysterious symbol later.

When the kids saw the Lincoln Memorial, they high-fived each other in excitement. Hundreds of people milled about while others sat on the step leading to the memorial. Avery was particularly excited to see the majestic white marble building. Her gaze traveled upward to the towering white pillars standing like soldiers guarding Abraham Lincoln's massive statue.

Jilly pointed up. "See those columns?" she asked. "There are 36 of them representing the 36 states in the Union at the time Lincoln died."

They started to climb the steps leading to the statue of Abraham Lincoln. Mimi, Papa and Sadie took the elevator. Evan counted the steps on the way up. "Fifty-six, fifty-seven, fifty-eight! I made it!" he announced.

As they entered the massive building, a feeling of reverence overtook Avery. She sensed that the statue was as monumental as the man himself had been. She touched a wall and found it cool to the touch. Mimi had explained earlier that many different types of stone were used to build the Lincoln Memorial. They had been transported from all over the United States. Mimi had said, "It was important to show that even a country torn apart by war could come together to build something spectacular and reunify the states."

Mimi, Papa, and Sadie strolled along, looking at excerpts from Abraham Lincoln's speeches inscribed on the walls. Avery, Ella, Evan, and Jilly stood at the base of the colossal statue of Abraham Lincoln. "That's just an amazing sight!" Avery exclaimed.

"I know," Jilly said. "It's hard to believe that the sculptor carved this statue by hand!"

Ella wiggled her fingers. "I can't even make stick figures hold hands," she remarked.

Avery got on her phone and looked up the statue. "This statue is made of Georgian marble and is 19 feet tall. Oh, and it weighs 175 tons. Wow—that's pretty heavy!" She continued to scroll down. "And get this, it was designed to face east, overlooking the reflecting pool and the Washington Monument."

Avery continued to research the memorial. "Hey, did you know that for 59 years, the Lincoln Memorial was on the back of the U.S. penny? Just a little trivia," she added.

Evan dug in the front pocket of his shorts, and shook some coins into his palm. He looked at the back of a penny. "Hey, wait a minute, the Lincoln Memorial's not on my penny," he said. "Why not?"

Avery laughed. "That's because in 2010," she explained, "a new penny was designed with the Union shield on it. It symbolizes how President Lincoln preserved the Union through the Civil War." She dug into the little purse strapped to her waist and handed Evan an older penny. "OK, no reason to look so sad. Now you have one."

"Thanks!" Evan said, flipping his new penny up and down. When the girls walked over to join Mimi and Papa, he moved to where the inscription of President Lincoln's second inaugural address was carved into the wall. He started reading, then stopped. The word that was supposed to read, "future" was spelled "euture." It looked like a correction had been attempted, but the mistake was still visible. Evan started to laugh. "Hey! You guys need to come and see this," he called.

But when he turned around, the others were gone.

"OK, not funny," Evan said, twirling in a circle to look for his family. They wouldn't have left him, would they? Would they?

Evan got a little panicky. The statue of Abraham Lincoln loomed above him, and he felt so small next to it. When he moved to the side of the statue, a shadowy hand waved at him from behind it. It pointed to a purple piece of paper lying on the floor. Terrified, Evan grabbed the paper and ran to find the others.

16

A REFLECTING POOL OF MYSTERY

Evan finally caught up with Mimi, Papa, and the girls. "Evan," Ella whispered, "where did you go? One minute you were here, and the next minute you were gone." She looked at his face. "What's the matter? You look a little pale." Evan was too embarrassed to tell her that he had gotten lost for a minute, but he did want to tell her about the note he'd grabbed. "Ella, I found another note!" he whispered.

Ella's blue eyes grew wide. "Really?" she asked. "Where? What did it say?"

"I-I don't know," he admitted. "An arm came out of the shadows and pointed to it. I just grabbed it and ran."

"Give it to me now," Ella said. He handed her the wrinkled note. She read:

TIME IS
RUNNING OUT!

"OK, kids, let's head down and see the reflecting pool," Mimi interrupted. "We only have an hour, so let's make the most of it." When she saw Evan's blank stare, she paused and put her hands on her hips. "Why, Evan," she said, "I'd think you'd be bursting at the seams with excitement to see your favorite place!"

More like burst into tears, Evan thought. He was still frightened from seeing that shadowy hand come out of the darkness. But he really did want to see the reflecting pool, so he stood tall and pulled himself together. "I want to go, Mimi!" he said. "Let's go!"

Evan headed down the stairs leading from the Lincoln Memorial to the reflecting pool. He counted, "Eighty-five, eighty-six, eighty-seven. Wow!" He shouted and made his favorite fist pump when he reached the reflecting pool. The girls laughed as he danced around in a circle and wiggled his skinny white legs.

Before them spanned the long, rectangular pool running from the Lincoln Memorial to the World War II Memorial. Without water in it, Evan thought it looked more like a skating rink than a pool. "Wow! Look how long it is!" he observed.

Ella stared at the bottom of the pool. "It's kind of creepy without any water in it, isn't it?"

Evan took a few pictures, then snapped his fingers. "Hey, I know," he said. "Since the pool is empty, we should be able to see the secret symbol, right? Come on, let's go look for it!"

The kids hurried to where they thought the center of the pool would be. But to their disappointment, the pool bottom was white, without a trace of a symbol. "Hmmm, that's really strange," Evan said. "The news guy said they could see the symbol from the air! What do you think?" He had faith that Ella could solve any puzzle.

Ella shrugged. "Maybe it can only be seen from the air."

"Maybe," Evan said. He wiped beads of sweat from his brow. "Gosh, it's hot!" he said, shading his eyes from the afternoon sun. He pulled a bottle of water from his backpack and gulped down some cool water. He stopped drinking when he thought he heard footsteps coming up behind him. He turned around and gasped. The two men were heading his way!

Evan didn't stop to think. He raced over to Avery, Ella, and Jilly. "Hey! Hey! Mr. Blondie and his friend are coming this way!"

The kids heard the crunch, crunch, crunch, of feet on gravel. "What should we do?" Jilly asked in a panicked voice.

"Get ready to run!" Avery cried. Just as the kids got ready to bolt, they heard Mimi's voice.

"Youuuu-Hooo, kids," Mimi called, waving at them with her white handkerchief. "Time to go! We must get to the Smithsonian Castle to meet Olivia. And Jilly, your mother just called. She is anxious to see you!"

The kids had never been so relieved to hear Mimi bossing them around. "Thank you, Mimi," Ella said. The kids raced to meet their grandparents and Sadie.

Mr. Blondie picked up a stone and threw it angrily into some bushes. "It's too hot out here to chase after those kids." Mr. Black Hair nodded, and they got into a waiting taxi.

17

A SMITHSONIAN CASTLE

Mimi, Papa, and the kids stared at the Smithsonian Building, known as The Castle, with its medieval-style turrets and towers. It really did resemble a castle of old.

"Look at that. It's a real castle!" Ella shouted.

The group entered the West Wing, known as the Chapel, just as Olivia came out of a door marked *Do Not Enter!* She clapped her hands in delight when she saw them. "Oh, how wonderful to see you all!" she exclaimed. She hugged Jilly, then said, "The portrait arrived early this afternoon. It really is marvelous. Mr. Tablebottom delivered it personally. You're just in time to see it before it goes on display for the celebration here tonight."

Mimi stared up at the cathedral ceiling. "What a lovely old building this is," she said. "I'll bet every single room is an architectural wonder!" Ideas for a mystery began percolating in her mind just by being in the castle.

"Yes, it is," Olivia agreed. "Completed in 1855, it was the first Smithsonian building. The Smithsonian is named after James Smithson." She cupped her hand near her mouth to whisper. "His crypt is inside the north entrance."

"Whaaaaatttt?!" Evan asked. "Why did people back then want to bury men in buildings?" He started walking like a zombie. "Watch out for the ghost of James Smithson!"

Mimi gave Evan a disapproving look and said, "Evan are you quite finished now?"

"Yes," he said, looking down at his feet.

"Thank you." Mimi turned to Olivia. "I am sorry for the rude interruption. Evan wishes to apologize. Right, Evan?"

"I am sorry, Ms. Carson," he said. "I should not have been disrespectful like that."

Olivia tried to hide her smile. "Now, as I was saying," she continued, "this building is currently used for administrative purposes, but they gave us a special area for the restoration. In fact, Mr. Tablebottom's assistant, Tara, insisted that we use this particular space." She led the group back through the *Do Not Enter!* door. Inside was a long hallway. "There are many corridors off this hallway," Olivia explained, "leading to separate chambers."

"What are the corridors for?" Ella asked, looking around while following the group single file.

Olivia shrugged. "All of them are unknown to me, except one," she replied. "It's Mr. Tablebottom's office. He took me there yesterday when the painting arrived. His office has its own entrance from the outside, so they brought the painting in that way."

She pointed out the corridor to them, and motioned to a small table and lamp. "This is how I remember where it is." She laughed. "I always fear I'll make the wrong turn and get lost in the castle."

The group entered a brightly lit room. A large painting was perched on the center of a table in a room enclosed by glass walls. The people coming and going around it wore surgical gowns and masks.

Evan was fascinated. "Why are they dressed like that? They look like doctors getting ready to do surgery."

Oliva smiled. "Restoration is a lot like surgery," she replied. "The restoration of an old painting is very serious work, and should only be done by a professional. Mr. Tablebottom has been restoring paintings for many years. His love of old paintings and sharp eye are why the Smithsonian commissioned him for such an important undertaking."

"Is that the painting?" Ella whispered.

"Yes," Olivia said. "They moved it from the Lockkeepers House this morning."

Evan tugged on Ella's sleeve. "Why are you whispering?"

Ella shrugged. "I don't know. It just seems like the proper thing to do here."

"Oh, OK," Evan whispered, then snapped a picture of the painting.

"All right, kids," Mimi said, looking at her watch. "We've taken up enough of Ms. Carson's time. She and Jilly need to get ready for tonight, and so do we. We'll see them at dinner before the ceremony."

The kids waved goodbye to Jilly. They were on their way out the door when Mr. Tablebottom entered the room. "Oh, Mr. Tablebottom, it's nice to see you again," Mimi said.

"Mmmm..." he said. His eyes were riveted on Evan's camera. "I would appreciate it if no one takes pictures in here," he said to Olivia, but eyed Evan as he went out the door. He gripped his hands into two tight fists and wanted to scream in frustration. *All my planning would have been for nothing if that kid had taken a picture. I have to get that camera!*

18

A BLUE CLUE

Ella watched as the elite of Washington, D.C., poured into the room known as "The Commons" at the Smithsonian Castle. She sat back in her chair, craning her neck to see the soaring vaulted ceiling. TV cameras were set up along the perimeter of the room, blocking some of the exhibition cases of rare artifacts lining the walls. Tables were set up with white linen tablecloths and red candles casting a golden hue over the room.

Mimi wore a dark green chiffon gown that cast shimmering waves in the candlelight. Papa looked dashing in his black tuxedo and cowboy hat. Evan was miserable in his navy blue suit and tie. He kept tugging on his collar. Avery looked adorable in her flowing, light blue dress. Rhinestones twinkled down the front as the lights shimmered on them.

Jilly entered the room with her mother. Olivia was dressed in a light yellow, floor-length sequined gown. Jilly wore a pink skirt and white ruffled blouse with pink and silver sequins dotting the front. She sat down next to Ella, who smiled brightly in her pink sleeveless dress with tiny sequins around the collar. "You look spectacular!" Jilly said as she sat down next to her."

"Back at ya!" Ella said.

Mr. Tablebottom entered the room. Tara walked a few feet behind him.

"There's something strange about that man," Mimi murmured.

"I agree," Papa said. "He's, uh, what's the word? Quirky?"

The group sat together at a large round table. A string quartet played soft music in the background while waiters served dinner. As Evan snapped pictures, Mr. Tablebottom glared at him. Ella saw the look and vowed she'd tell Mimi if he did it again.

Shortly after dinner, Mr. Tablebottom leaned over and lightly tapped Mimi's hand. She flinched. His hand was cold, just like a snake, she thought.

"I beg your pardon, Mrs. Marsh, but would you please tell Olivia I've gone to bring the painting out?" Mr. Tablebottom asked. Mimi nodded politely.

Soon, four men in white jackets wheeled the painting into the room. It was encased in glass to help preserve it. Olivia began her speech to kick off the event. "Good evening, ladies and gentlemen," she began.

Eventually, the painting was moved close to where the children were sitting to make way for dancing. Evan's seat was directly across from it. He glanced at it, then did a doubletake.

"Hey, wait a minute!" Evan whispered to Ella. "That's not the same painting I took a picture of before! Here, I have proof!" He searched for his backpack, then remembered that Mimi had asked him to leave it behind the reception desk during dinner. "Oh no," he lamented, "the SD card for my camera's in my backpack. I'll be right back."

Evan went behind the tall reception desk and quickly dug in his backpack for his SD card. He inserted it into his digital camera and scrolled through the pictures. He stopped when he saw the one he wanted. "Gotcha!" he whispered, and downloaded it onto his camera.

Suddenly, Evan heard footsteps. He crawled under the corner of the reception desk so he could peek around it. He couldn't see a person, but he recognized the snakeskin shoes and the creaking sound they made. "It's Mr. Tablebottom," he whispered. "But where's he going? Does he have the real painting hidden somewhere?"

Evan watched Mr. Tablebottom open the door marked *Do Not Enter!* Evan decided to follow him into the dark corridor, thinking he was a safe distance behind.

Mr. Tablebottom pretended not to hear Evan behind him. He kept on walking. *That kid has no idea I've been following him,* he thought. *I'll get that camera this time!*

19

A KEY TO THE MYSTERY

Avery, Ella, and Jilly stood near the painting waiting for Evan. A livelier band had started to play, so Mimi, Papa, and Sadie were dancing in a circle on the dance floor.

"Oh, oh, look," Ella said. "Tara's coming this way, and she doesn't look happy." She backed up against Avery and Jilly so they could huddle together. But to her surprise, Tara walked right past them. She stopped to speak with Olivia for a minute, then hurried out the door.

"Where's Evan?" Avery asked Ella.

"He went to get his backpack," Ella replied. "He said something about the painting being a phony, and that he had proof. Why?"

Avery started for the door. "Let's go find him," she ordered. "If he really has proof that the painting is a forgery, he could be in danger."

They didn't see Evan by the reception desk, but his backpack was there. "Now I'm worried," Avery said. "Evan's not here, but his backpack is. That's so not like him."

Ella saw the door marked *Do Not Enter!* slightly open. "Evan never closes any door. I think he went in there," she said. "Let's go, and stay together!"

As they entered through the door, Avery said, "OK, who else thinks this is a little scary?" She did not like sneaking around where they weren't supposed to be.

When they came to the desk and lamp Olivia had shown them earlier, Jilly pointed. "There's my mom's landmark!"

They turned into the dark corridor and walked until they came to an open door. "It must be Tablebottom's office," Ella said. She glanced inside. No one was there. A chair with two books on it sat against the far wall next to a door. Ella put her hand on the doorknob. "It's locked," she said. She motioned to the chair where the two books sat. "Avery, open one of those books and see if there's a key."

Avery gave her a look. But she opened the first book, and flipped through its pages. "Nothing here. Big surprise. You read way too many kids mystery books, sister dear."

"It's just funny that they're sitting right here on the chair," Ella said. "There's got to be something in one of them." Ella picked up the other book and shook it. CLINK! Something metal hit the floor. Dropping to their knees, they saw an odd-shaped little key. Ella picked it up and waved it in front of Avery's face. "See?" she asked. "You can never read too many kids mystery books, in my opinion."

"OK, OK," Avery said. "See if it opens the door before someone sees us."

Ella slid the key into the lock. It clicked. She let out the breath she'd been holding and opened the door. She peeked inside and saw a small winding staircase.

The girls crowded into the space. "I think this leads to one of the small towers on the corner of the main building," Jilly whispered.

Ella looked up the stairwell. "The door at the top is cracked open, and there's a light on in there!" She put her fingers to her lips to tell the others not to speak, and they tiptoed up the stairs.

20

BUSTED!

The girls heard voices coming from within the mysterious room.

"Gimmie that camera, kid!" Tablebottom shouted.

"I will not!" Evan said, clutching it to his chest.

Ella, Avery, and Jilly rushed through the door. "Don't you touch Evan!" Avery screeched.

Mr. Tablebottom whirled around. "Ah, you've come to rescue your brother. Well, it's too late!" He smirked at them. "What are you gonna do anyway? You're just a bunch of silly girls." He thrust out his hand to grab Evan's camera.

"STOP!"

Avery recognized Papa's booming voice. She and Ella whirled around to see Papa, Mimi, and Olivia standing in the doorway. Suddenly, Mr. Blondie and Mr. Black Hair appeared behind them, but now they were wearing green jackets. Tara was the last to enter.

"WHAT IS GOING ON IN HERE?" Papa's demanded.

"Papa!" Avery, Ella, and Evan ran to him for safety. Jilly clung to her mother.

Mr. Blondie and Mr. Black Hair pulled Mr. Tablebottom's arms behind his back and put handcuffs on him.

"How dare you!" He narrowed his eyes at Tara. "What is the meaning of this?"

"We know you tried to steal a valuable painting, Mr. Tablebottom," she said.

Ella pointed her finger at him. "Yes, he switched the painting with a copy! Then he tried to get Evan's camera to destroy any proof of the switch! He's a very bad man!"

"You're right, Ella," Tara said. "And you, Mr. Tablebottom, are under arrest." She nudged her head, and the two agents took him into custody.

"What do you know?" Mr. Tablebottom sneered. "You're just a meek little assistant."

Mr. Blondie and his partner snickered.

"What's so funny?" Mr. Tablebottom demanded.

Tara whirled on him. "I am Special Agent Tara Williams of the FBI. I work with a special bureau called the Protectors of the Mall!"

"You can't prove any of this," Mr. Tablebottom sneered.

"Yes, I believe I can," Tara said. She motioned for Evan to come forward to show her the pictures.

Evan flicked the photographs of the two paintings back and forth. "When Mr. Tablebottom painted the clock on the forged copy, he forgot there was no such thing as Daylight Savings Time during that period in history, so the clock is an hour ahead."

Mr. Tablebottom struggled against his handcuffs. "Yeah, well, I would have gotten away with it too, if it hadn't been for you meddling kids!"

"I seriously doubt that, Mr. Tablebottom," Tara said. "We had already moved the real painting through the secret tunnel under the castle to the National History Museum." She nodded at the agents. "Take him away."

Ella looked closely at the two men, who now had their backs to her. She gasped. "Evan, look on the back of their jackets. It says FBI!"

"We've been running from the FBI all this time?" Evan's blue eyes got wide. "Are we under arrest?"

"No, Evan, you are not under arrest," Tara said with a chuckle. "You are something of a hero!"

21

A PRESIDENTIAL THANK-YOU

Tara turned to Mimi. "Please accept my apology for getting you and your family involved in government business while you were here researching your new book."

Mimi graciously shook Tara's hand. "No apologies, needed, Tara. I am just so grateful you have protected my grandchildren!"

Tara nodded. "It was my pleasure, ma'am. I was originally summoned," she explained, "because the Lincoln Memorial Reflecting Pool was being drained. I just happened to stumble upon Alfred Tablebottom's plan to steal the painting. The FBI wanted to be sure we could implicate him in the plot. So, I was at the airport when he arrived to see where he was heading—and to see if he was working with someone here."

"Wait a minute," Evan said. "Why did you run away from me at the airport in the first place?"

Tara smiled. "I wasn't running from you, Evan. I saw Tablebottom, and I had to make sure he didn't see me until he met me here."

Avery asked, "We have been wondering something. How did you know where we were all the time?"

Tara held up her wrist. "My ID badge has a tracer on it. So, every time Evan was on the move, it beeped in my watch."

Ella held up one of the notes. "What about these? Was there any reason the notes were in different colors?"

"No," Tara laughed. "It's standard issue from our office."

Evan handed Tara her badge. "I hope it still works," he said. He blushed. "It was in my backpack for a while with all my other stuff."

Evan snapped his fingers. "Wait, that's it! That's where I'd seen that strange symbol before, the one the drone filmed on the bottom of the reflecting pool. It's on your badge!"

"Yes," Tara remarked. "It was very unfortunate that the drone picked up that symbol. The same symbol is on all the buildings we protect."

Tara took her ID badge and brushed some crumbs off. She held it up and examined it. "It seems to be OK," she said. "This badge gives me exclusive access to the national vault where special artifacts are stored." She secured a new retractable key ring to her badge. "I normally only wear it when I'm working at the vault. But that day, I forgot to take it off when I left."

"Why didn't you just get another one?" Avery asked.

"There are only seven people who have an ID badge like this one," Tara answered. "It contains a special microchip. In a state of emergency, all seven of us must be present to swipe our badges on a special keypad.

That procedure unlocks the underground passageways that run under the mall. If I ever lost my badge or it got into the wrong hands, I could lose my job, and maybe go to jail."

Ella stepped up. "Um, are you allowed to tell us what the symbol on your ID badge means?"

"It's the least I can do for having inconvenienced you kids so much," she said. She held up her badge. "The fountain represents the people. The swirls represent the three branches of our government. At the top is the executive branch, headed by the president. The two bottom swirls are the judicial branch, headed by the Supreme Court, and the legislative branch headed by Congress." She traced the swirls from one to the other. "Each part of the government is connected to the other. Each has its own responsibilities and powers that prevents one branch from gaining too much power over the other."

Avery nodded her head. "It's really cool to see a symbol like that for what I have learned in my government classes," she observed.

Tara shook each of their hands. "We at the FBI thank you, and the President of the United States thanks you for your bravery. Let us know the next time you're in Washington, D.C., and we'll give you a personal tour of one of the secret tunnels."

"Yessss!" Evan grinned and pulled his elbow down in his favorite fist pump. The girls giggled and hugged each other.

22

A
SPARKLER CELEBRATION

"Happy Fourth of July!" the kids shouted. Hundreds of people had gathered on the National Mall near the Lincoln Memorial to see the holiday fireworks. Families sat on the steps as children waved sparklers in the night air. Others waded in the Lincoln Memorial Reflection Pool's fresh, crystal-clear water. The air sizzled with excitement as the crowd waited for the fireworks to begin.

Evan swished his feet in the water along the edge of the pool. He was happy to see the Reflective Pool filled again. He glanced at his sisters and Jilly sitting on the edge of the pool with their feet in the water.

"I know what I'll do," Evan said to himself. "I am going to do a spin move to splash those girls!" Evan crossed his ankles to begin his spin, but his feet got tangled. "Whoooaaaaa!!" he yelled. He flailed his arms wildly to try to right himself before he splashed backwards into the water.

"Evan!" Avery and Ella yelled as water from his big splash cascaded over them. Evan looked up sheepishly, but his expression changed as he heard the crowd applauding and cheering.

"I'll give you a 10 for that one!" a man yelled.

"You only get a 9.5 from me," his friend called out. The crowd roared with laughter.

"OK, little brother," Ella said, walking back to their blanket on the grass nearby. "Don't look embarrassed. Just smile and wave like you do stuff like this every day."

"Wait," Avery said, "He does do stuff like this every day!"

"I'm not embarrassed!" Evan exclaimed. "I think they like me!" He waved his sopping shoes in the air and took a big bow.

Mimi leaned her head on Papa's shoulder. "Look at that," she said. "I think we have just created a star right here in Washington, D.C.!"

The End

Join the Fan Club at
CaroleMarshMysteryClub.com and...

Enter to win
our monthly prize giveaways

1

2

Get status updates
from Mimi and the characters

View the library
of Carole Marsh Mystery titles

3

4

Read
the first 3 chapters of any mystery book for FREE

Download
free activities to go along with your reading adventures!

5

GLOSSARY

aggravate: to annoy or exasperate someone

ambassador: an official sent by a government to represent a temporary mission

hunkered: crouched down low

melodious: pleasant-sounding

mischievously: playfully annoying

pompadour: a man's style of hairdressing in which the hair is combed into a high mound in front

quivered: trembled from cold or from strong emotion

relevant: having something to do with something happening or being discussed

SAT GLOSSARY

abdomen: the body space between the chest and pelvis that contains all the digestive organs, including the stomach, small and large intestines, pancreas, liver, gallbladder, kidneys, and spleen

aghast: overwhelming shock or amazement

implicate: to fold or twist together

intrepid: fearless, determined, set in purpose

oscillate: to move back and forth

Enjoy this exciting excerpt from:

THE MYSTERY

AT

Hilton
Head
Island

1

THE HINKY DINKY

"There it is! There it is!" Avery, Ella, Evan, and Sadie shouted. They stood on the deck of the *Hinky Dinky*, a boat that ferried passengers from Palmetto Bluff across the May River and into the Calibogue Sound each day. What they had spotted on the shore was the famous red-and-white-striped Harbour Town Lighthouse.

"Is there anything prettier than a lighthouse?" Ella asked, her hair whipping in the breeze. Her grandmother Mimi nodded.

"Or more romantic?" swooned Avery, her eyes wistful. Mimi nodded again.

"Or *spoooooooookier?*" suggested Evan, with a grin.

Everyone stared at the boy, who clasped the bobbing deck railing with white knuckles.

"Why spooky?" asked Ella in aggravation. "It's bright daylight and as far as I have ever heard, this lighthouse is not haunted." This time, Mimi smiled.

Avery looked startled. "Is it, Mimi? Is the lighthouse haunted?" She sounded hopeful.

"No!" Ella insisted. "Mimi brought us over to Hilton Head Island to have fun for a change—NOT to chase some ghost or mystery—right, Mimi? If you wanted to do that, you would have brought Grant and Christina." But Grant and Christina were getting older and had more important things to do this summer than solve mysteries (or so they said).

"Miiiiiiimiiiii?" Evan said in a teasing voice. "Tell us now. Tell us the truth."

Mimi stood on the bow of the boat, waiting for it to dock at the marina. She did not smile. She did not frown. She did not purse her lips the way she often did when she hesitated to tell her grandchildren something. Instead... she screamed!

2

PORPOISE SISSIES

"Where's Sadie?" cried Mimi. Her red sundress flared as she twisted left and right to look for her youngest granddaughter. "She was right here! She was walking Coconut." Coconut was Mimi's little white rescue puppy that she took everywhere, even on airplanes.

The children scattered to search for their five-year-old sister. Surely she had not fallen overboard? All the kids were good swimmers. Sadie could swim the length of their pool at home without taking a single breath.

Avery soon spied a glint of strawberry-blond hair bouncing in the breeze. Sadie stood with Captain Young at the stern of the boat. She squealed as dolphins jumped over the bow wake like wet, gray **parentheses**.

"Look! Look!" Sadie cried when she spotted her family heading toward her. "Porpoise sissies!"

"That's *porpoises*, Sadie," Ella corrected.

"They're manimals," Evan added.

"That's *mammals*," Ella corrected again. Evan stuck out his tongue.

"Besides," said Avery, "they are actually dolphins." Captain Young nodded in agreement.

"That's enough!" said Mimi, racing up to her granddaughter. "Thank you, Captain, but I'll take her from here." Mimi adored her four youngest grandchildren, but she found keeping up with them a handful. They never seemed to stay together in one place for long.

Sadie was so excited about the "porpoise sissies" that she let go of Coconut. The dog tore around the deck, dragging her red leash behind her.

Avery just stood there, **stoic**, ignoring the usual **ruckus**, and took in the scene before her. They were coming into port at the famous Sea Pines, home of the also-famous Heritage Golf Tournament and the beautiful Harbour Town Lighthouse. As the noonday sun glinted off the waves, the green grass, the blue sky, and the storybook white puffy clouds, she sighed.

"Mimi," Avery said, tugging at her grandmother's arm. "This looks like a book cover to me. You did come here to write a mystery, didn't you?"

Now that everyone was accounted for, Mimi looked at her beautiful granddaughter and winked. "You don't think I came all the way over here on this lumpy-bumpy water just to eat lunch and shop, do you?"

Avery laughed. "No! But, uh, I sure hope we *are* going to eat lunch and shop."

"And climb the steps to the top of the lighthouse?" Evan butted in.

Mimi groaned. The one thing she could be sure of was that each of her grandchildren would want to do something different while they were at Hilton Head—and all of them would exhaust her!

With a jolt, the *Hinky Dinky* bumped into the wharf. Helpful deckhands tied the lines up to cleats. In a moment, the gangplank was lowered and they all walked, scampered, hopped, or skipped off the boat.

"That felt just like being a pirate!" Evan said, with that one-eyed squint he always had in the bright sun. "Made me feel just like Jack Wheelbarrow."

"Jack Sparrow," corrected Avery.

"No, Jack Bonemarrow," teased Ella.

"Where did the porpoise sissies go?" lamented Sadie, looking back at the water.

"DOLPHIN!" her brother and sisters yelled together.

Sadie folded her arms, stomped her foot, and ran to find Mimi, who was talking to Captain Young.

"Hey, you guys," Avery whispered. "Mimi said she IS going to write a mystery!"

Ella groaned. "And we are surprised?" She swiped her sweating forehead with the back of her hand.

"Then we'd better help her," said Evan. "You know she counts on us to..."

"To what?" asked Mimi, coming up behind them, hand in hand with Sadie and cradling Coconut in her other arm.

"Uh, to, uh...be good while we're here?" said Evan. His sisters giggled.

"Well, I could try to count on that," said Mimi with a sigh, "but I know better!"

Suddenly, Avery turned toward the town. "Do I smell hushpuppies?!"

Mimi laughed. "Was that sound I heard the sound of growling tummies?"

All four kids rubbed their stomachs and nodded.

"Then we'd better head to the Salty Dog right away!" Mimi said and herded the gang of kids forward off the dock and into the quaint village.

As the girls ran ahead, Evan lagged behind, muttering, "I don't want to eat a salty hot dog. I want shrimp and hushpuppies."

As usual, no one paid Evan any mind... except for the last passenger off the boat, who seemed determined to keep an eye on the young boy and his family.

3

THE SALTY DOG

The Salty Dog Café was just the kind of place the kids loved Mimi to take them to for lunch.

"Ah, outside tables with umbrellas," said Ella, as she plopped onto a deck chair.

"Aha!" said Evan. "I see fried shrimp and hushpuppies, and boy, am I hungry!"

The waiter took their order and the kids settled back; they knew what came next. Never, ever, had they gone anywhere with Mimi that she did not give them a mini-history lesson. It was never boring and often helped them solve the mystery that always seemed to be afoot.

Avery pulled out a map she had picked up at the front counter and unfurled it. She laughed. "Hilton Head looks like a foot!"

The other kids peered over her shoulder. The island was indeed shaped like a foot, with a heel, a sole, and a toe.

"And we are right here on the toe," said Ella.

"Can we go to Skull Creek?" begged Evan, pointing to another spot on the map.

"Where's the salty doggie?" asked Sadie.

"And why do they call it Hilton HEAD, when it looks like a FOOT?" Evan wondered aloud.

"Can I get one of those Salty Dog tees, Mimi?" pleaded Avery.

"Can I get my fingernails painted in red-and-white stripes like the lighthouse?" Ella asked.

Mimi ignored her grandchildren. She sat quietly, sipping her iced tea with lime and mint. When the kids grew quiet, she began.

"A *head* also means a point where land meets sea, especially where you can have a good lookout, say, for invaders. We're having *dinner* at Skull Creek. We *will* get tee shirts in the gift shop before we leave. And I *love* the idea of red-and-white-striped fingernails and toenails!"

As she spoke, the waiter brought their food, and ketchup was squirted all around. Sadie munched on her "salty dog" hot dog. While everyone ate, Mimi gave them some background.

"Hilton Head got its name from an English explorer—Captain William Hilton—who came here to map the coastline," Mimi explained. "His ship was called the *Adventure*. He spotted this point of land, which was named Hilton's Head, after him."

"And later, Hilton Head Island?" guessed Avery.

Her grandmother nodded and continued. "You've studied the 13 original colonies in school. Well, the colonists had to find ways to make a living. They built ships here, and later they established many plantations, where rice, cotton, indigo, and other crops were grown—with the help of slaves."

"Slaves?!" said Evan.

"I'm afraid so," said Mimi. "But after the Civil War, the slaves were freed. Hilton Head became a quiet island. People hunted, fished, and harvested trees for lumber. After a bridge was built to connect the island to the mainland, tourists began to come over to enjoy the wide, sandy beaches."

"Just like we do every summer!" said Ella.

"And they built the lighthouse so ships wouldn't run aground?" asked Avery.

Mimi laughed and nodded. "You can see its light 15 miles out to sea. But mostly I think it's famous because everyone loves it, and a famous golf tournament is played here each year—the Heritage. As a matter of fact, it starts soon."

"Can we go up in the candy cane after lunch?" asked Sadie, a ring of ketchup around her mouth.

"Yes, we can!" said Mimi, wiping Sadie's face. "And our history lesson will continue there."

The kids groaned.

With so many people in the café and tee shirt shop, it was not surprising that the kids did not spot the man from the boat still trailing them. While everyone else wore shorts and tee shirts and flip flops, the man looked out of place in his trench coat and slouch hat. In fact, he could not have looked more suspicious if he tried. And that made him *very* suspicious!